Silky the Fairy enters the Land of Mine-All-Mine from the Faraway Tree looking for adventure. She has visited many Lands in search of fun and excitement. But when she meets Talon the evil Troll she soon finds that her Enchanted World is turned upside down.

To rescue the Talismans that have been lost from the Faraway Tree, Silky will need some help, and fast! Luckily she can rely on her best fairy friends to help her in her task. With the special talents of Melody, Petal, Pinx and Bizzy, Silky must save the Lands of the Enchanted World. But will the fairies succeed or will Talon get his evil way?

EGMONT

We bring stories to life

Silky and the Rainbow Feather
Published in Great Britain 2008
by Egmont UK Limited
239 Kensington High Street, London W8 6SA

Text and illustrations © 2008 Enid Blyton Ltd, a Chorion
company
Text by Elise Allen
Illustrations by Pulsar Studio (Beehive Illustration)

ISBN 978 1 4052 4254 7

1 3 5 7 9 10 8 6 4 2

A CIP catalogue record for this title is available from the British
Library

Printed and bound in Great Britain by the CPI Group

Enid Blyton's ENCHANTED WORLD

Silky and the Rainbow Feather

By Elise Allen

EGMONT

Meet the Faraway Fairies

Favourite Colour – Yellow. It's a beautiful colour that reminds me of sunshine and happiness.

Talent – Light. I can release rays of energy to light up a room or, if I really try hard, I can use it to break out of tight situations. The only problem is that when I lose my temper I can have a 'flash attack' which is really embarrassing because my friends find it funny.

Favourite activity – Exploring. I love an adventure, even when it gets me into trouble. I never get tired of visiting new places and meeting new people.

Favourite Colour – Blue. The colour of the sea and the sky. I love every shade from aquamarine to midnight blue.

Talent – As well as being a musician I can also transform into other objects. I like to do it for fun, but it also comes in useful if there's a spot of bother.

Favourite activity – Singing and dancing. I can do it all day and never get tired.

Favourite Colour – Green. It's the colour of life. All my best plant friends are one shade of green or another.

Talent – I can speak to the animals and plants of the Enchanted World . . . not to mention the ones in the Faraway Tree.

Favourite Activity – I love to sit peacefully and listen to the constant chatter of all creatures, both big and small.

Favourite Colour – Pink. What other colour would it be? Pink is simply the best colour there is.

Talent – Apart from being a supreme fashion designer, I can also become invisible. It helps me to escape from my screaming fashion fans!

Favourite Activity – Designing. Give me some fabrics and I'll make you something fabulous. Remember – If it's not by Pinx . . . your makeover stinks!

Favourite Colour – Orange. It's the most fun colour of all. It's just bursting with life!

Talent – Being a magician of course. Although I have been known to make the odd Basic Bizzy Blunder with my spells.

Favourite Activity – Baking Brilliant Blueberry Buns and Marvellous Magical Muffins. There is always time to bake a tasty cake to show your friends that you care.

www.blyton.com/enchantedworld

Contents

Introduction

*T*ucked away among the thickets, groves and forests of our Earth is a special wood. An Enchanted Wood, where the trees grow taller, the branches grow stronger and the leaves grow denser than anywhere else. Search hard enough within this Enchanted Wood, and you'll find one tree that towers above all the others. This is the Faraway Tree, and it is very special. It is home to magical creatures like elves and fairies, even a dragon. But the most magical thing about this very magical Tree? It is the sole doorway to the Lands of the Enchanted World.

Most of the time, the Lands of the Enchanted World simply float along, unattached to anything.

But at one time or another, they each come to rest at the top of the Faraway Tree. And if you're lucky enough to be in the Tree at the time, you can climb to its very top, scramble up the long Ladder extending from its tallest branch, push through the clouds and step into that Land.

Of course, there's no telling when a Land will come to the Faraway Tree, or how long it will remain. A Land might stay for months, or be gone within the hour. And if you haven't made it back down the Ladder and into the Faraway Tree before the Land floats away, you could be stuck for a very long time. This is scary even in the most wonderful of Lands, like the Land of Perfect Birthday Parties. But if you get caught in a place like the Land of Ravenous Toothy Beasts, the situation is absolutely terrifying. Yet even though exploring the Lands has its perils, it's also exhilarating, which is why creatures from all over the Enchanted World (and the occasional visiting human) come to live in the Faraway Tree – so they can travel from Land to Land.

Of course, not everyone explores the Lands for pleasure alone. In fact, five fairies will be asked to do so for the ultimate cause: to save the life of the Faraway Tree and make sure the doorway to the Enchanted World remains open. These are their stories . . .

Chapter One

The Land of Mine-All-Mine

'There's a new Land coming to the top of the Tree!'

Silky the Fairy's long, blonde hair soared behind her as she whizzed down through the Faraway Tree's branches and leaves, dappled with every shade of green imaginable. She beamed as she flew, her wings fluttering excitedly and her blue eyes shining in her pretty face. Nothing thrilled Silky like the arrival of a new Land, and every time Cluecatcher told her that one was coming, she buzzed with so much excitement she couldn't contain it. Now she was whizzing through the Tree shouting out the good news to everyone: Dido the Dragon, Dame Washalot, Moon-Face, Gino the Giant . . . every creature, up and down and all around the Tree's massive trunk. Nothing could dampen her enthusiasm; not even the Angry Pixie throwing open his shutters and giving his usual opinion about 'loudmouthed fairies'.

Silky was nearly all the way back up the Tree when she saw a lanky, pointy-eared sylvite boy (with the handsome face, dark blue eyes and silver hair that all sylvites are known for) gently brushing and cooing to a gorgeous, snowy-white winged unicorn.

'Zuni!' she cried to the boy.

She flew up to her best friend and Misty the Unicorn, who whinnied in welcome.

'I'm just going to take a wild stab in the dark,' Zuni laughed, taking in Silky's flushed and excited face. 'There's a new Land coming to the top of the Tree.'

'The Land of Mine-All-Mine!' Silky enthused. 'And it'll be here any minute – come on!'

'The Land of Mine-All-Mine?' Zuni wrinkled his nose. 'I don't like the sound of it. Maybe you should skip this one.'

'That's what you said about the Land of Ghosts and Ghouls and remember what happened there? I had a lovely time,' Silky retorted.

'I know, but –'

'But what?' Silky insisted, 'It could be anything. That's

what's so exciting about a new Land. You never know what you'll find there. Come with me.'

'I will,' Zuni replied, 'tomorrow. Today I promised Misty we'd ride through the Enchanted Wood, and then I –'

Silky stopped him, shaking her head. 'I can't wait until tomorrow. What if the Land moves away by then?'

'It probably won't,' reasoned Zuni. 'Anyway, you shouldn't go on your own. The Land of Mine-All-Mine doesn't sound like the friendliest place in the Enchanted World.'

'Oh Zuni,' Silky said, rolling her eyes.

'I'm serious, Silky,' argued Zuni, giving her one of his stern looks. 'What if something happens to you and there's no one around to help?'

'I'll be fine. I'm only going to take a quick peek. I'll see you when I get back!'

Before he could say anything else, she gave her wings a mighty flap and soared to the top of the Tree. It was kind of Zuni to worry about her, but totally unnecessary. Silky was well on her way to visiting every single Land in the Enchanted World, and she'd never had a problem. Well, there was that time in the Land of the Wicked Wizards when she'd been trapped and almost didn't get away ... At least, she'd never had a problem she couldn't handle perfectly well on her own.

At last she reached the Ladder at the top of the Faraway Tree. She was nearly at the new Land! Her stomach fluttered in anticipation. What would she find in the Land of Mine-All-Mine? What kind of creatures would she meet? It was thrilling, entering a brand new Land for the first time, each rung of the Ladder bringing her closer to all its mysteries, and Silky never got sick of it. Her body gave an involuntary shiver as she pushed through the thick, moist cloud at the very top of the Ladder, until finally she emerged ... into the middle of a public square, teeming with masses of arguing goblins, ogres and trolls, all of whom were shouting at each other.

As she looked around, Silky noticed menacing 'KEEP OUT' signs everywhere. Leaning in closer, Silky read 'Property of Bluebeard', 'Property of Ebenezer' and 'Property of Harpagon' on the nearest signs. Then one voice sounded above all the rest of the shouting crowd behind her.

'Look!' cried a goblin, making Silky whirl around. 'A *fairy*!'

Everyone from the Land of Mine-All-Mine froze mid-sentence to stare at Silky.

Silky smiled her friendliest smile. She was always ready to give new creatures the benefit of the doubt, even ugly goblins and trolls. But there was something about the way these creatures were looking at her that Silky didn't like. Something . . . *hungry*.

'*She's mine! All mine!*' a young ogre

screamed, and hurled himself at Silky.

The rest of the crowd followed, all of them lunging at Silky, grabbing her hair, her dress, her wings as they screeched over and over again:

'Mine!'

'*Mine!*'

'ALL MINE!'

It took less than a second, and suddenly there were fingers, claws and pincers from a thousand different creatures, all grabbing at

her, tugging at her, as the voices howled in her ears: 'Mine!', '*Mine*!', 'MINE!' She tried to get away, but they grasped at her wings and she couldn't take off. 'Mine!', '*Mine*!', 'MINE!', they yelled.

Silky couldn't move. There were so many creatures, she felt as if she couldn't breathe.

'Stop!' she cried, struggling to escape the endless grabbing fingers. 'Stop it! Get off me!'

'*Let the fairy go*!' boomed a deep voice.

And just like that, the crowd backed away, shuffling to clear a corridor for a hulking troll, larger than all the rest. Even bowed by deeply hunched shoulders, he towered over Silky and she felt the strength of his grip as he took her hand in both of his.

'Forgive them,' he asked her with a wide smile. 'It's been a long time since we've had any visitors.'

'Really?' Silky asked, lifting her chin and fixing the crowd with her most piercing glare.

'I can't imagine why.' She looked pointedly at her captured hand. 'Now, if you'll excuse me . . .'

But the Troll ignored her.

'As far as I know, there are only two ways for visitors to arrive here,' he began, licking his lips. 'By magic, or from the Faraway Tree. Tell me, which one did you use?'

'The Faraway Tree,' Silky replied, all her attention focused on getting away from the Troll's vice-like grip. 'Now really, thank you for your help but please let go of my hand. I'd like to leave, so . . .'

'Oh, you'll leave,' the Troll said.

His voice was suddenly so vicious that Silky shuddered with fear. The Troll's teeth were now bared and he began to spit out words in a foreign language. Silky saw a large crystal around his neck flash once . . . and then everything around her went blank.

Chapter Two

Talon the Troll

'Ow!' Silky yelped as something banged against her foot.

She tried to reach down to it, but she couldn't move her arms. They were bound to her sides by a chain. In fact, her whole body was wrapped in the chain. She couldn't move at all, except for a constant bouncing and jouncing. Was she on a train?

Silky looked around, but saw only dark fabric and . . . a glint of silver. That must have been what hit her foot. It was a coin, she realised, squinting to get a better look, but it was the largest coin she'd ever seen – about the size of her head! What was going on?

Silky looked up and saw the Troll's face towering above her like a gargantuan statue.

She was in his pocket! His forehead and nose gleamed with sweat and from the way Silky was being bounced around it felt as if the troll was climbing downwards. Utterly stunned, Silky stared, transfixed, as a bead of sweat on the tip of the Troll's nose billowed . . . bloomed . . . and fell right on top of Silky, drenching her from head to toe.

'Ugh!' Silky cried, disgusted.

She shook the sticky Troll-sweat off her face and tried to think rationally about her

situation. Obviously, the Troll had shrunk her. She was in his pocket and he was taking her somewhere. She needed to escape. The chain around her was both thick and tight, but she could easily break free with her fairy power: illumination.

By simply concentrating, Silky could glow as softly as a flickering match, or with a ray of light so hot and powerful that it could knock down a brick wall or break through a thick chain. All she had to do was focus . . . but she couldn't. That was the problem with Silky's power. If she was feeling sad or uncertain, she couldn't illuminate. And at that moment, Silky felt absolutely horrible. How could she have let this happen? She should have been more alert; she should have seen this coming; she should have –

THUMP! Silky fell backwards as the Troll bumped to a stop.

'Can I help you?' said a familiar voice.

fore Silky could identify the speaker, the Troll's monstrously large hand reached in, grabbed her and thrust her forwards. It only took a second for Silky to realise that they were at the very bottom of the Faraway Tree, and Elf Cloudshine was standing directly in front of them. (There were always two elves stationed here at the foot of the Tree, although Silky had never known why.)

'Cloudshine!' Silky screamed. 'It's me, Silky!'

Although her shrunken voice could only make a tiny squeak, Cloudshine's eyes grew wide and frightened at the sight of her chained and gripped tightly in the Troll's fist.

'You *can* help me,' the Troll hissed. 'You can let me into the Vault, or I'll crush this fairy like an insect!'

Cloudshine put out a hand and spoke to the Troll gently. 'Let's not do anything rash,' he said.

Silky saw the elf's other hand subtly

∗ 16 *∗*

reaching for the wand at his side . . . but the Troll had seen it too.

'Drop the wand!' he snapped. 'Any hint of magic and I will crush your friend!'

He squeezed Silky hard and, despite herself, she squealed. Cloudshine released his wand at once.

'Leave her alone,' he said hastily. 'I'll open the Vault.'

'*No!*' cried Silky.

She didn't know what was in the Vault, but she was quite sure that admitting the Troll would be *very* bad. She scanned the area — was there anyone else around to help her? Zuni? Dido? Even the Angry Pixie would be a welcome sight. But there was no one.

Apart from the elves, Witch Whisper was the only creature who lived at the bottom of the Tree. Silky could see her now, through the windows of her ramshackle cottage. The old crone was hunched in her rocking chair, her back to Silky and the drama outside. She wouldn't be any help. All Witch Whisper ever seemed to do was sit in her rocking chair, humming to herself.

A low, grumbling roar grabbed Silky's attention. The ground beneath the Tree was moving and swirling like a whirlpool. Finally it caved in on itself to reveal a perfect circle of golden light, which was so bright that Silky had to look away. One of the Tree's roots became smooth and metallic as it stretched into the glistening abyss, and the Troll leaped on to it.

'Thank you,' he said to Cloudshine. Then, almost as an afterthought, he added, 'Oh – just in case you wanted to go for help.'

The Troll recited a quick spell and the crystal around his neck flashed. Silky cried out in horror as the bark of the Tree trunk rippled, bubbled and then grew over poor Cloudshine's head and body like a blanket. The Troll popped Silky back into his pocket and . . . WHOOSH! They slid down the root, faster and faster and faster, hurtling deep underground as if they were on a log flume.

Silky was still chained up, but she managed to stand and peek out of the Troll's pocket. At first the golden glare stung her eyes and she had to look away. However, when her eyes had adjusted, what she saw made Silky's jaw drop.

They were speeding through a long, tube-like chamber that seemed to stretch on for an eternity. In the walls were circle after circle of everyday objects, each in its own special nook. It was these objects that were giving off the golden glow. Despite the danger she was in, the beauty of the objects filled Silky with a sense of wonder.

THUMP! The Troll landed on the ground and Silky clung to the edge of his pocket. He beamed up at the glowing objects, and Silky

thought that his triumphant smile was even more grotesque than his sneers.

'And now,' he declared, 'I fulfil my destiny and make the entire Enchanted World mine . . . *all mine*!'

He laughed – a mirthless, greedy sound that echoed through the chamber. Then he started to chant in the same strange language that he had used before.

As the Troll chanted, Silky felt something powerful churning inside her. She was furious. Not with herself – not any more. She was angry with the Troll. He had used her to get to the Faraway Tree and break into the Vault, and now he was doing something terrible to these wonderful, glowing objects. Silky could feel their energy reaching out to her, crying out for help. Her anger grew until, like a volcano, it exploded out of her in a burst of bright, powerful light.

'AAAHHH!' she screamed, shattering her

chains with the power of her white-hot light.

Silky struggled to free herself from the Troll's pocket, shooting her dazzling rays all the way to the top of the Vault and beyond. The very walls shook with the power of her radiance, but the Troll only laughed.

'You're too late, little fairy!' he cried triumphantly. 'My spell is almost complete!'

Horrified, Silky could see that the objects were shimmering in their nooks, already fading into oblivion.

Suddenly, Silky heard a high-pitched screech from above. Looking up, she saw a giant, bird-like shadow diving straight towards her. Silky shrieked and covered her face with her hands, bracing herself for the attack.

But the attack never came. As the shadow swooped close, Silky realised that it wasn't a bird at all, but a person. It was an old woman, lined and wrinkled with centuries of wear, although her sapphire eyes flashed with the

ferocity of youth. She soared down the Vault on outstretched arms, her deep-blue cloak flapping around her like wings.

The Troll sneered at the sight of the old woman, then raised his voice and continued his spell, his eyes burning. Silky realised that the old woman was reciting a spell too. The two voices, both speaking strange languages, seemed to be battling with each other as they echoed through the chamber.

Silky hauled herself out of Talon's pocket and on to the floor. The glowing objects began to flicker and fade, and the powerful whine of the hovering woman's spell competed with the Troll's howling chant.

And then the objects disappeared.

'*No!*' gasped Silky.

'NO!' snarled the Troll, baring his teeth at the old woman. 'Witch Whisper!' He spat out the name as if it were poison in his mouth. 'How dare you? Those were mine! All *mine!*'

'You should have known better than to come back here, Talon,' said the old woman. 'And *that* belongs to me.'

She pointed at the crystal necklace, fixed him with a baleful stare and began a new spell. Talon the Troll's eyes widened in fear. He quickly hugged himself tight, muttered in his own magic language and then vanished in a puff of smoke, leaving Witch Whisper and Silky alone in the cavernous vault.

As soon as he had gone, the fire went out of the old woman's eyes. She floated down to the ground and leaned wearily against the wall. Gingerly, the still-tiny Silky flitted closer and looked her in the eye.

'Witch Whisper?' she asked, still hardly able to believe what she had just seen.

The old woman nodded.

'But I thought . . . we all thought . . .'

'That I was nothing more than a crazy old crone?' Witch Whisper asked, a playful gleam in her eyes. 'I know the Tree people have made me a fairytale monster. I've been around a very long time, Silky. Too long, I'd have said just yesterday. Living in this Tree all this time. Feeling useless.' She smiled and added, 'But then you called, and I knew I had more to give.'

'*I* called?' Silky asked, puzzled.

'With your light,' Witch Whisper explained. 'It burst all the way into my cottage. Blew my door off its hinges, to be perfectly honest.'

Silky blushed. 'I'm sorry,' she said.

'Don't be – it got my attention,' said Witch Whisper. 'Without that light, the Talismans would have been lost forever.'

'Talismans?' Silky repeated.

Before Witch Whisper could answer, she and Silky heard a clear but distant CRACK! It was followed by a loud yowl that grew louder and closer until they heard a thud and a groan.

Witch Whisper turned to Silky with a look of grim determination.

'I think it's time I introduced myself to the rest of the Tree,' she said. 'Come on!'

Chapter Three

The Tale of the Talismans

The noises that Silky and Witch Whisper heard had come from Gino the Giant. His tree branch had snapped, plummeting both Gino and the branch to the ground. This was unheard of – the branches of the Faraway Tree could support *twenty* giants and had done so on several occasions.

Moments after Gino's accident, Dido the Dragon had seen three leaves falling from the Tree – an absolute impossibility! Faraway Tree leaves *never* fell. Shortly after that, Cluecatcher, whose powerful nose and multiple eyes enabled him to tell which Land was at the top of the Tree, had burst into piercing wails. He was upset because the Lands of the Enchanted World suddenly felt 'fainter' to him. What could it possibly mean?

Word of these terrors spread quickly through the Tree and panic soon followed. Silky (whom Witch Whisper had returned to her usual size) gathered every single Faraway-Tree resident for an emergency meeting. Even the sudden appearance of the witch didn't seem to surprise the residents – they were too frightened.

Under a slow but alarmingly steady trickle of falling leaves, Silky told the residents what had happened.

'But I still don't understand,' Silky finished, turning to Witch Whisper. 'Who is Talon? And why did he want everything in the Vault?'

'And what about the falling leaves?' the Angry Pixie cried out.

'And my branch,' bellowed Gino the Giant, who was nursing a bump on his head.

'Is – is the Tree sick?' stammered Dido the Dragon, puffing out a ball of smoke.

Everyone had questions and soon there was a noisy babble of worries, fears and accusations, with no one listening to anyone else. Finally, Witch Whisper inserted two fingers into her mouth and blew the shrillest whistle anyone had ever heard. There was an instant and surprised silence.

'I'll explain everything,' said Witch Whisper. 'Cluecatcher – is the Land of Mine-All-Mine still at the top of the Tree?'

Cluecatcher's enormous head, which was much larger than his body, tilted upwards. His radar-dish ears spun from side to side, his eight eyes peered into the sky and he took a giant sniff with his powerful nose.

'It's gone,' he said. 'Another Land will be here soon, but I can't yet tell which one.'

'Then I need to be quick,' Witch Whisper said, taking a deep breath. 'A long time ago, several of us came together to make a portal – a sort of gateway – to the Lands of the Enchanted World, so that all creatures could travel to different Lands and enjoy them.

'We took ordinary objects from each Land, such as a ballet slipper from the Land of Dance, a goblet from the Land of Revelry, a mop from the Land of Extreme Cleanliness. We filled these objects – these Talismans – with the spirit of their Land, then secured them in a Vault deep beneath the ground.

'The combined energy of these Talismans

was so powerful that it created life. The Faraway Tree sprouted around them, and so the Talismans are the life force of the Tree. We were all very proud of what we had done, but one of us became greedy and wanted the portal for himself. He knew that if he controlled the portal, he could control the entire Enchanted World.'

'Talon,' Silky realised with a gasp.

'The Troll that *Silky* brought to the Tree!' the Angry Pixie screamed.

'Stop it!' interjected Zuni. 'This isn't her fault.'

'Please,' Witch Whisper held up a hand and everyone fell silent again. 'Yes, it was Talon. We stopped him before he could steal the Talismans and exiled him to an abandoned Land, one with no Talisman, which would never bring him near the Faraway Tree.

'Only after he had gone did we realise that he had stolen one of my crystals. Talon didn't know how to use it at the time, but we knew that one day he might learn, and, if he did, he would find a way back. But after so many uneventful years, I thought we were safe. I was wrong.'

'And now . . . Talon has the Talismans?' Zuni asked, a deep frown on his handsome face.

'No,' said Witch Whisper. 'His spell was weak; it was simply a wish in Trollish made on a stolen crystal. No match for the magic of a true witch.'

'But I saw them disappear,' Silky objected.

'I couldn't reverse Talon's wish – it had gone too far when I arrived,' replied Witch Whisper. 'But I was able to change it. I sent the Talismans back to the Lands they came from. They're safe.'

'Great!' said Zuni. 'So just magic them back into the Vault and everything will be OK.'

The crowd murmured in relief and agreement, but Witch Whisper gave a weak smile.

'The Talismans are immune to magic when outside the Vault,' she said. 'It is for their own protection.'

'But you said the Talismans are the life force of the Faraway Tree,' Silky said slowly. 'If the Talismans are outside the Vault . . .'

Witch Whisper nodded.

'If nothing is done, the Faraway Tree will perish and the portal to the Enchanted World will close forever,' she said.

There were at least a hundred creatures gathered for the meeting, but every one of them was silent. The idea of the Faraway Tree dying, of their whole community having to leave, of never visiting another Land again – it was too terrible to bear. Even the Angry Pixie's eyes welled with tears.

But Silky perked up, sensing hope. 'You

said, "if *nothing* is done". That means something *can* be done.'

'Yes,' Witch Whisper agreed, 'there is something, but it's very dangerous. Someone must go into each Land as it settles on top of the Tree and bring back its Talisman. I need to stay here to protect the Tree in case Talon should return.'

'I'll do it!' Silky offered at once.

'It won't be easy,' Witch Whisper warned, looking carefully at Silky. 'The Talismans could be anywhere in the Lands and held by anyone – possibly a very unfriendly anyone. Talon will also be after the Talismans, and he won't be kind to those who get in his way.'

Silky took a deep breath.

'I understand the dangers, but I want to do it,' she said. '*I'm* the one who brought Talon here. I want to be the one to make it right.'

'And I want to come with you,' Zuni said, stepping forward.

Silky smiled gratefully at her friend, but Witch Whisper shook her head.

'It's too dangerous,' she said.

'Too dangerous for me and not for Silky?' scoffed Zuni. 'I don't think so.'

'Silky can fly,' Witch Whisper replied. 'You can't.'

'Since when has that made a difference?' Zuni retorted.

'It could,' said Witch Whisper. 'In a tight situation, a partner who can't fly could be disastrous for Silky.'

'Fine,' said Zuni, sounding frustrated, 'So I'll take Misty. *She* can fly.'

Misty whinnied, nodding and pawing the ground in agreement.

'Zuni, Misty is a flying unicorn,' said Silky gently. 'She's the last of her kind. Do you really want to endanger her like that?'

Zuni paused just long enough for Witch Whisper to step in.

'Silky's right,' she said. 'It's too dangerous for Misty. I'm sorry Zuni, but it's best if Silky does this on her own.'

'But . . . what if Silky can't do it?' Gino asked quietly. 'I mean, no offence, Silky, we all love you, but . . . what if you can't?'

Silky looked out at the hushed crowd. Countless pairs of pleading eyes were looking to her for reassurance and hope. What could she tell them?

'I won't let you down,' Silky vowed. 'Nothing will stop me from returning every single Talisman to that Vault. I promise.'

After the meeting had broken up, Witch Whisper asked Cluecatcher and Silky to stay behind. The minute the next Land arrived, Silky would begin her mission. Zuni remained as well, pacing back and forth.

'Am I the only one who thinks this is a terrible idea?' he said. 'Silky shouldn't have to do this all by herself. What if she gets into trouble?'

Cluecatcher suddenly perked up, his eyes, nose and radar-dish ears pointing up at the sky. He inhaled deeply.

'The new Land is about to arrive,' he said, then sniffed again. 'Fairyland.'

Silky felt a thrill rush through her body.

The next Land was Fairyland – her home!
She hadn't been there in decades. (Fairies have
a much longer life span than human beings,
and in fairy years, Silky was still a girl.) Her
mind raced, thinking of everything she had
left behind: her parents, her room, her four
best friends, Pinx, Berry, Petal and Melody . . .
just the thought of them made her smile. They
were all completely different, but absolutely
inseparable. If ever there had been a perfect
team . . .

Silky broke into a huge smile.

'That's it!' she cried, turning to Zuni. 'Zuni,
for once you might actually be right. If
everything works out as I hope, I won't have
to do this all by myself after all!'

Chapter Four

Melody

S ilky made her way up the Faraway Tree and through the cloud. With a giggle of delight, she soared into Fairyland. It felt incredible to be back in this beautiful and familiar place: the lilac sun peering through the lemon clouds that streaked the soft pink sky; the acres of spun-sugar fields with their pastel patchwork of poofling puff blooms; the rushing majesty of the River-rise Rapids; the stunning purple skyriver that ducked and darted through the clouds. As she flew, she fingered her heart-shaped crystal pendant, which Witch Whisper had enchanted just before Silky had left.

'The closer you get to a Talisman, the redder the crystal will grow,' Witch Whisper had told her.

Right now the crystal remained perfectly clear. Her first stop was her parents' home in Everwell Valley, just outside Fairyland's main city, Fairyopolis. Her father, Chrysos, and her mother, Lumella, were overjoyed to see her and very proud to hear about her mission. They were worried for her safety, of course, but Silky had inherited her confidence from her parents. If she believed she could successfully get all the Talismans back to the Vault and defeat Talon, her parents believed it too. Chrysos and Lumella were thrilled to hear that Silky's plans included her old friends, and they told their daughter exactly where she could find each one of them.

Soon, Silky was zipping over the turquoise mountains of the Tremolo Trail, which led to the Conservatory, the home of the Twinkletune Fairies. While all Twinkletunes were known for their skills in the musical arts, most had only one area of expertise: they could either dance, sing or play instruments. However, according to Chrysos and Lumella, Melody excelled at all three disciplines and her talent eclipsed all others. It was said that a song from Melody could mend a broken heart and her dance could bewitch the cruellest monster.

Although Silky hadn't seen Melody for a long time, she didn't think it would be difficult to recognise her friend. She could picture Melody perfectly in her mind: the long orange hair pulled

back in a ponytail, the
large green eyes, the
graceful dancer's body ...

Silky arrived at the
Conservatory and her
breath caught in her
throat.

'Oh ... dear ...' she
groaned.

The Conservatory was
a giant tower, stretching
higher than the eye
could see. It was divided
into countless rooms
within which hundreds
of Twinkletunes danced,
sang and played
instruments. Silky peered
into window after
window and each time,
she saw fairies with

long orange hair pulled back in a ponytail, large green eyes and graceful bodies. *All* of them! How was she ever going to find Melody amidst these look-alikes who were spinning and dancing in perfect unison?

'Excuse me?' Silky called out to the nearest fairy.

The fairy showed no intention of stopping her mad pirouette. She whirled towards Silky, who screamed and ducked out of the way.

It was the same all the way up the tower. At every level, Silky was bombarded by lilting voices, stirring instrumentals and eye-boggling choreography, all performed brilliantly by what seemed like a sea of Melodys. They were all so engrossed in their music that they didn't even notice Silky, let alone stop to tell her which one was the *real* Melody. By the time Silky neared the top of the Conservatory, her head was spinning. Clearly, getting her old friends to help was going to be harder than she had thought.

That was when she heard the song. It was the most stunning, moving tune she had ever heard in her life. There were no words; they weren't needed. The melody alone brought tears to Silky's eyes. Hypnotised, Silky flew to the top of the Conservatory, where a lone Twinkletune perched on a vine-covered musical note. She strummed a luquellute and swayed gently in time to her song, her orange ponytail swishing behind her like a graceful dance partner. All other thoughts emptied from Silky's mind as she watched and listened, perfectly entranced.

'Silky!'

Even Melody's shriek sounded musical, but at least it was jarring enough to break Silky out of her trance. She beamed as Melody flew to her and the two friends joyfully hugged.

'I'm so glad you're here!' Melody enthused in her tinkly voice. 'Can you stay for dinner?

We should have a picnic! At the beach! Oh, I
know the most beautiful spot. It overlooks the
ocean and you can hear the call of the
whaloons and –'

Silky had to laugh. 'Melody,' she interjected,
'I haven't seen you in ages. Aren't you at all
curious why I'm here?'

Melody thought for a moment, then
shrugged. 'Nope. I'm just glad you are.' She
linked an arm through Silky's. 'So . . . what

would you like to do first?'

Silky just beamed. There were many reasons why she had always loved Melody, but her sunny personality was certainly near the top of the list. Still, Silky had come here on serious business, and it would have been dishonest to pretend otherwise.

She cringed inwardly as she told her friend the story, already imagining Melody's enthusiasm fading as she heard about Talon, the Talismans and all the dangers involved in bringing them back. Even as she spoke, Silky wondered at her own nerve, popping back into the lives of four long-ago friends only to drag them into a dangerous adventure that had nothing to do with them ...

'I'm in!' Melody chirped.

'What?' Silky stammered. 'Really? But ... I told you it could be really dangerous, didn't I?'

'It's not too dangerous for you, right?' said Melody. 'So it's not too dangerous for me. And besides, we'll be together. And we'll see all kinds of wonderful new places. Don't you see? It'll be absolutely magical!'

Silky's head was spinning – Melody was trying to convince *her*! Still, she had to make sure Melody understood what she was getting into.

'OK,' she said, 'but you know there's no guarantee we'll succeed . . .'

Melody just cocked her head and looked at Silky. '*You* think we'll succeed, don't you?'

'Well, yes, of course I do, but –'

'Then that's all I need to know!' Melody beamed. 'When do we start?'

Silky laughed, completely caught up in Melody's enthusiasm. She told her friend to meet her at Everwell Valley in the morning, where hopefully they'd be joined by the rest of their old gang.

'I can't wait,' declared Melody, giving Silky a huge hug. 'Thank you,' she added as she pulled away. 'I'm honoured you thought of me.'

Silky just shook her head in amazement at Melody's unfailing optimism. She gave her friend a final grateful hug, then took off for the Fairyland Farms to find Petal.

Maybe this wouldn't be so hard after all.

Chapter Five

Petal

'I don't think so,' Petal cooed. 'I don't think that's a good idea at all.'

Silky stopped in her tracks. Had Petal read her mind?

Silky had only just arrived in Fairyland Farms, where Petal lived with her Uncle Delta. Uncle Delta had recognised Silky at once and, smiling, had pointed her towards the fields. Silky found Petal sitting alone, staring at some roses. Nearby in the pasture, a cow lazily chewed the lilac Fairyland grass. Petal had always been at home with plants and animals, so it wasn't surprising for Silky to find her perfectly happy, just sitting there. What *was* surprising was Petal's reaction. Silky hadn't even said hello, and yet Petal was

already turning her down.

Silky was about to turn away, when Petal spoke again.

'Honestly, I think you owe me an apology,' she said. 'Don't you?'

Did she? Silky was stunned; this wasn't at all how she had imagined the conversation would go. She hadn't even said a word! But clearly Petal somehow knew what Silky wanted and, if Petal felt she deserved an apology, then . . .

'I'm . . . I'm sorry,' Silky stammered.

Petal whipped around, a shocked expression on her face. Then her green eyes softened.

'Silky?' she asked.

'Yes,' Silky replied, more confused than ever. 'But . . . you already knew that. I mean, you answered my question . . . not that I'd actually asked it, but . . .'

Petal laughed – a deep, soothing sound that

came from her very core.

'Oh, Silky,' she said. 'I wasn't talking to you at all. I was talking to Madame Rosita!' She wrapped Silky in a warm embrace. 'It's good to see you, Silky. It's really been too long.'

But Silky was still looking around for Petal's partner in conversation.

'Madame Rosita?' she asked. 'Petal, I don't see any–'

Petal brushed her bobbed, red hair back from her face and indicated the largest, most beautiful rose.

'This,' Petal declared, 'is Madame Rosita.'

Although no breeze blew, the flower seemed to shiver slightly and Petal turned on the bloom.

'Stop it, Madame Rosita. I will *not* tell her that.'

'Tell me what?' Silky asked, and then realised what she was saying. 'Wait – you can actually *talk* to that flower?'

'To all plants and animals,' Petal explained.
'It's a power that grew after we saw each
other last.' She shot a warning look at
Madame Rosita, and then added, 'Sometimes
I'm not sure if it's a blessing or a curse.' To
Madame Rosita she said, 'Stop it and be nice.'

'What?' asked Silky, terribly curious as to
what a rose could be saying.

'Believe me, you don't want to know,' Petal
assured her.

Of course, that only made Silky *really* want
to know!

'What?' she urged, 'What did she say?'

Petal sighed, unwilling to lie, but clearly
unhappy about sharing the information.

'She doesn't like your tiara,' Petal admitted.
'She thinks you're trying too hard to be
beautiful. She says real beauties like her never
need to adorn themselves.'

'What?' Silky cried, her hands flying to her
tiara. She turned on the giant bloom, her

indignation growing by the second. 'How dare you? I'll have you know, I'm not *trying* to do anything with this tiara. I just happen to like it, and I don't care what anyone else thinks, least of all some run-of-the-mill rose! Why, I –'

'MOOO!'

The cow had moved closer and seemed to want to add her voice to the argument. Silky spun around, her face flushed with anger.

'Oh really?' said Silky. 'Now *you* want to criticise me too?'

'Actually,' Petal said in a soothing tone, 'Amelia was standing up for you. She and Madame Rosita almost never agree.'

'Oh,' Silky said, feeling a bit silly for yelling at the cow. 'Well . . . you have my apologies then. Thank you, Amelia.'

'That's what I was doing when you arrived,' Petal explained. 'Refereeing between the two of them. Madame Rosita seems to think it's beneath her to be planted so close to

Amelia's ... droppings –'

Amelia mooed plaintively and Petal turned to her soothingly.

'I know, Amelia, but it's what she said.' Petal leaned towards Silky and added, 'Amelia's very sensitive about the topic, as you can imagine.'

Silky wasn't sure she could, but decided it was best to go along with it.

'Of course,' she said.

'Anyway,' Petal continued, 'Madame Rosita threatened to uproot herself in protest, which I thought was a terrible idea and horribly disrespectful to both Amelia and myself.'

'Ohhh,' said Silky, now understanding perfectly ... or as much as it was possible to understand a conversation between an old friend, a sensitive cow and a diva of a rose.

'But enough of all this,' said Petal, taking Silky's arm and leading her away from

Amelia and Madame Rosita (who were still squabbling, judging from the steady stream of moos). 'What brings you back to Fairyland?'

Silky told her everything. Petal visibly shuddered as Silky described what was happening to the Faraway Tree – its branches breaking and its leaves falling. Before Silky had even finished, Petal put up a hand.

'Stop,' she pleaded, 'I can't take any more. What Talon is doing to the Tree . . . whatever it takes, I want to help you save it.'

Silky was touched by her friend's concern for the Tree, but she knew that Petal should hear the whole story. She explained that they needed to travel to all the Lands of the Enchanted World and gather the Talismans, beginning right here in Fairyland. Petal grew quiet and Silky allowed her to think. There was a long silence.

'I do want to help you,' said Petal eventually, 'and it would be a dream come

true to meet all the different plants and
animals of the Enchanted World . . .'

There was another long silence.

'But . . . ?' Silky urged.

'But I've never been away from Fairyland,'
Petal said. 'And I feel so tied to this Land and
the creatures here . . . I don't know if I can
leave.'

'You don't have to,' Silky assured her. 'I
understand.'

'No, I *want* to,' Petal protested. 'I just . . . I'll
help you find the Talisman here. As for what

happens next . . . maybe I can decide that later.'

That was good enough for Silky. The two friends hugged, and Silky told Petal about the meeting the next morning in Everwell Valley. Then she flew off to find Pinx.

Chapter Six

Pinx

'Pinx!'

'*Pinx!*'

'PINX!'

The cries made Silky's ears ring. She had arrived at Pinx's Fairyopolis fashion studio only to find herself in a mad crush of fairies, all screaming for attention as they teemed around the studio's closed door.

'Ow!' Silky winced as someone's toe knocked into her ear. 'Hey!' she added, as someone else's fluttering wing pummelled her nose.

It was impossible to function inside this frenzied hive. Silky was just about to give up when the door flew open.

'Enough!' screamed Pinx, her electric-pink, zigzaggy pigtails shooting out of the top of her head like lightning bolts. 'You all have to wait your turn – or else!'

She scrunched her eyes shut, balled up her fists and concentrated until . . . she disappeared into thin air. Pinx's fairy power was invisibility.

The crowd gasped, then cried out, '*Pinx*!' in horror.

When the group was good and worried, Pinx reappeared several metres away.

'See what happens?' she warned them. 'You abuse the Pinx, you lose the Pinx.'

Pinx's expression suddenly changed as she spotted Silky in the crowd.

'*Silky*!' she cried delightedly and yanked her friend out of the crush.

'Hi,' said Silky. 'I suppose you're wondering why I'm here . . .'

'Of course not,' said Pinx. 'I know *exactly* why you're here and I can't believe you didn't come sooner! Come on!'

Pinx whisked Silky into the studio and shut

the door behind them, muffling the protests of
the frustrated crowd left behind.

'You *know* why I'm here?' Silky asked,
confused.

'Of course!' Pinx cried. 'Same reason as
everyone else. You heard about the
commission and you want a dress. But you

should know that I've been booked solid for months. I'm only squeezing you in because you're my friend.'

As Pinx spoke, she dragged Silky on to a pedestal, one of eight in the room. The others were all occupied by fairies wearing wild pink gowns – riotous explosions of feathers, bubbloons, pufflepoofs and ruffellettas. Young fairies fluttered around the customers, pinning,

prodding, folding, adjusting and constantly looking to Pinx for approval. However, Pinx was concentrating only on Silky.

She flitted up to a high rack of fabric rolls and peeled off a length of shimmering pink sequinolined silk, which she draped around Silky's body and over one shoulder.

'Arms up,' Pinx ordered.

Silky obeyed. There was really no other choice.

'What commission?' Silky asked, but Pinx only rolled her eyes.

'Silky, it's *me*,' she said, reaching into a bowl of pink sweets and popping a handful into her mouth. 'You don't have to pretend you didn't know and you just *happened* to come by to see an old friend. I'm happy to do this for you, really. Arms down.'

Silky lowered her arms and Pinx scrunched her lips to one side, concentrating, then grabbed several giant pink blooms and sewed them on to a strap to make a sash.

'I'm serious, Pinx,' Silky insisted. 'I don't even live here any more. I live in the Faraway Tree, and –'

'*Please*,' Pinx interrupted, 'I don't care how far away your tree is – *everyone* knows I was commissioned to make Princess Twilleria's gown for her Sweet Centennial ball tomorrow –'

Silky screamed. She couldn't help it – this was huge news!

'You were?' she cried. 'Pinx, that's fantastic! Congratulations!'

She grabbed Pinx in a giant hug, but Pinx quickly pulled away.

'Don't crush your flowers!' she warned, then cocked her head, studying the elated Silky. 'You really didn't know?'

'No!' Silky insisted. 'That's what I was trying to tell you! I haven't been in Fairyland for ages. I live in the Faraway Tree and I wanted to see you because . . .' her voice trailed away as she recognised one of the fairies on the other pedestals. 'Is that *Marisolode*?' Silky asked, amazed.

Marisolode was the most famous movie star in all of Fairyland.

'Mm–hm,' Pinx beamed. 'I'll introduce you if you want. She's very nice but she's also *very* demanding.'

Pinx reached back into her bowl of sweets but stopped short before popping them into her mouth.

'Excuse me!' she called out to the room. 'Why do I have a blue Choco-Bite? I only want *pink* Choco-Bites! *Pink!*'

Instantly, an apologetic assistant flew over and whisked away the offending sweet bowl, swapping it with a perfectly pink replacement.

'So, as I was saying,' Pinx continued, 'she is *very* demanding.'

Silky had to suppress a giggle but Pinx

didn't notice.

'I've had celebrities, royalty . . . you saw the crowds out there," said Pinx airily. 'Everyone who's anyone wants *me* to design their ball gown. It's everything I always knew would happen for me.'

Pinx stood back, admiring her work on Silky's dress.

'I've done it again,' she proclaimed. 'It's perfect.'

Silky spun to look at herself in the mirror. The dress was a cacophony of different shades of pink. The skirt exploded out from Silky's waist, twice as long on one side than the other. The bodice bubbled at the front and poofed at the back, and the shoulder straps blossomed with blooms. It was spectacular.

'Wow,' Silky gushed.

'If you're quite finished,' Marisolode called over from her pedestal, 'I've been *waiting* here . . .'

Pinx just rolled her eyes and kept her attention on Silky.

'So tell me,' Pinx urged, 'if you didn't know about the commission, why did you come to see me?'

Silky paused. Pinx was living her dream. Would she even care about Talon, the Talismans and the Faraway Tree? There was only one way to find out. Silky told her the whole story – quickly, since Marisolode wasn't the only customer who was getting impatient.

'So when I heard Fairyland was at the top of the Tree, I thought of my oldest friends and how amazing they were,' Silky told Pinx. 'I knew that if anyone could handle the challenge –'

'It would be me!' Pinx finished, her eyes glowing with pride.

'Well, yes,' Silky agreed. 'You, me and the rest of our old group: Melody, Petal and Berry –'

But Pinx was already imagining her new biography.

'This will be huge for me,' she said. 'I mean, I'm already huge in Fairyland, but this kind of exposure ... we'll be going everywhere! I can see the headlines: "Pinx – Saving the Entire Enchanted World from Evil Trolls and Bad Fashion". And when we've finished and we come back, we'll be heroes! They'll make a movie of our lives!' Pinx gasped. 'Marisolode can play me!'

'So ... you'll come?' asked Silky.

'OK, here's the plan,' Pinx declared, ignoring Silky's question, 'I have to work, so you talk to the other girls and make sure they're in. Then we need a meeting place ...'

'How about tomorrow morning in Everwell Valley?' Silky suggested with a grin.

'Perfect,' agreed Pinx. 'I'll see you there.' With that she zoomed off, calling, 'Marisolode! You won't believe this – I have

the most *amazing* project for you . . .'

Silky just smiled. Three down, one to go . . .

Chapter Seven

Berry or Bizzy?

S ilky loved her new Pinx-designed dress, but while it was perfect for a ball, it was a bit over the top for flying around Fairyland, so she dropped it off in Everwell Valley before heading off to Spelling Square, where Berry lived.

Spelling Square was wholly devoted to young Conjurer Fairies like Berry. Every shop advertised a list of magical classes, and the alleys teemed with young fairies trying out their skills and older mentors seeking out the perfect apprentices.

For Conjurer Fairies, this spirit of competition made Spelling Square exciting. For all other fairies, it was a crazy place that was best avoided. Silky had never been to

Spelling Square before but, based on the stories she had heard, she thought it wise to settle herself on a stone gargoyle at the very top of one of the student apartments. The lofty view would give her the best chance to spot Berry, and hopefully she would be out of the way of any stray spells.

Then the gargoyle started to talk.

'I say,' it blustered, 'I think it's the absolute *height* of rudeness to sit on someone's head.'

'Aaah!' cried Silky, jumping into the air. 'I'm so sorry, I . . .' She paused for a moment. 'Aren't you made of stone?'

'Oh, and I suppose you think that means I have no *feelings*?' snapped the gargoyle. 'Well, I'll have you know, little lady –'

He got no further because, just as suddenly as he'd come alive, he turned back into stone, except that now he was facing Silky and sneering at her. Silky decided to move.

She flitted down and perched on a lamp

post, but within minutes a passing Conjurer had turned it into an eagle and Silky had to leap off its back before it flew away with her. Spelling Square was exhausting! If she didn't find Berry soon . . .

'*Berry*!' Silky cried, spotting her friend flying above her.

Berry hadn't changed a bit. As always, she was neatly put together, her black hair held perfectly in place by a demure headband that matched her simple dress and shoes. The only jewellery she ever wore was a watch on a plain brown band; anything else was far too frivolous for her. Even as a child, Berry had been exceptionally serious about everything. Of course, that meant she was just as serious about her friendships and therefore incredibly loyal.

Silky zoomed up to Berry and wrapped her in a hug . . . but Berry didn't hug her back. In fact, Berry seemed to be looking around as if she were worried about who might be watching. However, Berry had always been reserved, so Silky didn't mind.

'It's so good to see you!' Silky enthused.

'Yes, it's good to see you too,' Berry agreed . . . in an unenthusiastic kind of way. 'Look, Silky, I'm really busy, so −'

'You?' Silky declared with a grin. 'I don't believe it − you could never be *Bizzy.*'

Berry looked at her seriously for a second and then laughed, finally relaxing into the girl Silky used to know. Berry's younger sister, Bizzy, had been the bane of the girls' existence when they were growing up − the ultimate little-sister pest. Berry and Bizzy couldn't have been less alike. Silky and Berry laughed, remembering how Bizzy used to cast spells in the middle of their games to mess them up.

'Like the time she conjured a mud puddle under our game of leap-squog!' Berry remembered.

'The worst!' Silky agreed. 'Remember how we'd scare her away with pretend cans of "Bizzy repellent"?'

In perfect sync, the two girls held up imaginary aerosol cans and made spraying sounds as they pretended to use them.

After they'd stopped laughing, Berry said, 'I'm sorry. It's been wonderful seeing you, Silky, but I really have to go.'

'Just give me a few more minutes,' said Silky. 'There's something I have to ask you.'

Silky told Berry all about Talon, the Talismans and the Faraway Tree, and how she hoped to get her old friends together to save the Enchanted World. Berry listened closely to the whole story and, finally, she nodded. Silky's heart leaped – Berry was in!

'I see what you're saying,' Berry mused, 'but I really don't think the life of one little tree is that important.'

Silky couldn't have been more stunned if

Berry had hit her over the head with an elephant (which was entirely possible in Spelling Square).

'"The life of one little tree"!' she repeated incredulously. 'But it's more than that. If Talon defeats us, the lives of everyone in the Enchanted World will be threatened!'

Berry cocked her head and thought about it, nodding again as she worked it over in her head.

'No,' she declared eventually. 'I still don't think it would affect *my* life enough to make it worth the risk. Thanks for asking though. It was great seeing you.'

And with that, Berry flew off without a glance behind her. Silky stared after her in disbelief.

'But . . .' she stammered.

'You . . .' she tried again.

'AAAHHH!' she cried in frustration, bursting into a flash of light.

'Try not to let her bother you,' a soothing voice urged.

Silky turned to see a chillingly ugly cockroach, half the size of her foot. It was standing on the building nearest to Silky and waggling its antennae as it spoke. Silky screamed and kicked out at it with her shoe. The enormous cockroach rubbed its hideous head with a repulsively hairy leg.

'Ouch,' it said. 'That hurt.'

It leaped off the wall and started to fly towards Silky, who began to back away in terror, until . . .

'Sorrysorrysorry!' called a girl's voice. 'Massive Magic Mistake. I tried to send a cock*atoo*, but it came out cock*roach*. Basic Bizzy Blunder.'

The voice muttered a quick counter-spell, the cockroach disappeared in a puff of smoke and Silky turned to see . . .

'Bizzy?'

Not that she really needed to ask. There was no mistaking Berry's younger sister. The two looked exactly alike . . . except for the fact that they looked completely different. Unlike Berry's perfectly straight tresses, Bizzy's black mane curled out in all directions. Her dress had gloriously clashing colours. And while Berry prided herself on her unadorned neck, ears and wrists, Bizzy's bevy of bangles clangled and jangled with every move she made.

'Yes, it's me,' Bizzy admitted, 'and I sort of, accidentally-on-purpose overheard what you and Berry were saying . . .' Bizzy thought for a second and then added, ' . . . which I suppose makes me a Bizzy-body!'

She laughed at her own joke but when Silky didn't join her, she stopped.

'I just want to apologise for my sister,' continued Bizzy. 'She's got this *thing*, this very-Berry-never-merry, all-about-me *thing*. She only thinks about getting an apprenticeship with the top teacher in Spelling Square, and nothing and nobody else.'

'Yes, that was the impression I got,' Silky sighed, then smiled at Bizzy. 'Thanks.'

She took off, eager to leave Spelling Square.

'Wait!' cried Bizzy, rushing to catch up with her. 'Let me take her place!'

'What?' asked Silky.

'On the Talon-Trouncing, Talisman-Toting team!' Bizzy bubbled. 'I want to help! You're trying to save the entire Enchanted World. And I'm just as good a magician as Berry. Even better.'

Silky couldn't help but smile. 'And the cockroach that was supposed to be a cockatoo . . .?'

'Mini-Mistake,' Bizzy grinned. 'But it got your attention, right? Try me. I'm not the same fairy you knew when we were younger.'

It was true; Silky could tell. Bizzy had the same crazy energy she'd had when they were younger, but there was strength behind it now. Besides, there were bound to be some tough times ahead; the group could use a Conjuring Fairy – and a little craziness to keep them going.

'It's a deal,' Silky said, and told Bizzy about the meeting the next day in Everwell Valley.

'*Yes!*' celebrated Bizzy, wrapping Silky in a hug. 'I promise you won't be disappointed!'

Suddenly, a cloud seemed to fall across her face, and when she spoke again her voice was small.

'Are you sure everyone else will be OK about having me on the team?' she asked.

Silky gave her an encouraging smile.

'I'm positive,' she assured Bizzy. 'It won't be a problem at all.'

Chapter Eight

The Perfect Team?

'This is a *problem!*' shrieked Pinx, pointing an accusing finger at Bizzy. 'If she's in, I'm out!'

For the first time in decades, Silky's friends were gathered together. So far it was not going very well.

'Pinx . . .' Silky cajoled.

'Why?' cried Bizzy.

'Are you kidding?' retorted Pinx. 'You were such a pest!'

'That's not fair!' snapped Bizzy. 'Remember this?'

She held up an imaginary aerosol can and made spraying sounds as she pretended to use it. Melody giggled and Bizzy turned on her, aghast.

'It's not funny!' she cried.

'OK, but let's be fair,' Silky protested. 'You weren't very nice to us, either.'

'Exactly,' said Pinx with a challenging glare. 'How about the time you popped a swarm of bees into the middle of our Fairy in the Dell circle?'

'The bees were not happy,' Petal said, shaking her head.

'The *bees* weren't happy?' Pinx yelled. 'We were almost stung to death!'

'I don't know that we need to shout about this,' Melody reasoned.

'"Stung to death"?' said Petal, wrinkling her nose. 'Pinx, I think that's a *bit* of an exaggeration . . .'

Pinx turned on her. 'Why are you defending the bees?'

'The bees were an accident,' Bizzy explained. 'I was trying to make *fris*bees, which would have whizzed all around and been fantastically funny. Something just went a little wrong with the spell — a Basic Bizzy Blunder! But I'm much better now. Look — I'll make us some dandelion cider: Cida-lida-mite-a-chita-chooder-ooder-ooder!'

Bizzy threw her hands out in front of her and POOF! A massive, eight-legged creature skittered wildly all around the fairies. Silky, Pinx and Melody screamed in horror.

'That's not cider, it's a *spider*!' Melody shrieked.

Bizzy winced. 'Oops. Minor Magic Mistake.'

'*Minor?*' Silky cried as the hairy spider crept her way, threatening to crawl on to her foot. 'AAAHHH!' she screamed. 'Squash it!'

'Silky!' Petal gasped in horror.

'*Bizzy, do something!*' Melody screeched as the spider headed towards her. Bizzy raised her arms again and POOFED the spider away.

'See?' Pinx wailed. '*This* is why we don't want her on our team.'

'Because she doesn't think spiders are horrible creatures?' Petal asked indignantly. 'I don't think that's fair at all. In fact, after that display, I don't know if I want to be on a team with the rest of you.'

'Maybe we're all just getting a little too emotional . . .' Melody said.

'Yes,' Petal agreed, taking a deep breath. 'Melody's right. What if we make a list of the good and bad things about Bizzy, and then we can make a solid decision.'

'I don't want to make a list,' snapped Pinx, throwing her hands in the air. 'Let's just say what we think. I say No Bizzy. Melody, what about you?'

Melody looked as if she wanted to disappear. She hated confrontation.

'I'm not really comfortable deciding that . . .' she stalled.

'Well *get* comfortable!' Pinx urged. 'If we're going to be a team, we're going to have to be honest about what we think. So, Melody, what do you think?'

Pinx waited for a response, but got none. In fact, Melody was no longer there.

'Melody?' said Pinx.

All the fairies looked down.

On the spot where Melody had been standing, there was now a small, porcelain music box. A ballet dancer who looked like Melody was twirling on a platform as a tinkling tune played.

'Oh no,' Pinx groaned.

Melody's fairy power was transformation. By simply concentrating, she could turn herself into anything – provided she knew the object well. The skill was extraordinary . . . but she used it mainly to escape uncomfortable situations.

'This is crazy,' Pinx objected. 'Is this going

to happen all the time?'

'Mm-hm,' Petal nodded. 'I absolutely agree with you.'

'You do?' Pinx asked happily.

'Oh no,' Petal said, 'not you. I was talking to the irises. They said you're being completely unreasonable and insensitive, and I happen to agree.'

She nodded behind her, where a patch of irises did seem to be looking at Pinx in a rather judgemental way.

'Don't bring the plants into this, OK?' asked Pinx.

'You just don't like the fact that they're right,' snapped Bizzy.

'I just don't like the fact that they're *plants*!' retorted Pinx. 'Fine – that's *it*!'

Pinx clenched her fists and made herself invisible.

Silky's head was spinning. She had truly believed that she and her old friends would make the perfect team, but it all seemed to be going wrong. She felt the pressure building inside her until she couldn't possibly contain it any more; until it had to burst out of her.

'AAAHHH!' she yelled at the top of her voice.

A bright ray of light WHOOSHED out of Silky, illuminating the entire horizon, blowing back the grass, the irises and the fairies' hair. Silky felt as if she no longer had

any control. All her thoughts came out in a mad, screaming rush.

'Listen to you!' she yelled. 'Look at you! Melody's a *music box*, for fairy's sake! Pinx has vanished! Petal's talking to the flowers and Bizzy . . . I don't even know *what* Bizzy's doing!'

'Actually, I –' Bizzy started, but Silky cut her off.

'I don't care!' she cried. 'The point is, right now Talon could be on his way to snatch the Fairyland Talisman, taking his first step towards controlling the entire Enchanted World, and I'm not doing anything about it because I'm too busy watching you act like *spoilt children*!'

Chapter Nine

The Rainbow Feather

Everyone was stunned by Silky's outburst. Pinx and Melody returned to their normal selves. They all stared at Silky, and there was a long silence.

Then they burst out laughing.

'Silky's had a flash attack!' Melody giggled.

'Her first since she's been back,' Petal added.

'I've never seen an Illuminating Fairy before,' Bizzy marvelled. 'Does that happen often?'

'Only when she's *really* upset,' Pinx said. 'You caught a good one.'

'I'm glad this is so amusing to you,' Silky said with a frown.

However, the corners of her mouth were

curving upwards as she began to see the funny side of her tantrum.

'OK then,' said Petal. 'What do we have to do to get this Talisman before Talon does?'

Petal, Bizzy, Pinx and Melody looked at Silky for an answer. Silky was flummoxed.

'That's it?' she asked. 'Everything's OK now? You're all in?'

The fairies all exchanged glances and nodded – of course they were in.

'I made Duchess Eleanorian change her fitting schedule so I could be here with you lot,' Pinx grinned. 'If that's not "in", I don't know what is.'

Silky beamed, looking at her team.

'OK then,' she began. 'Our first mission is to find Fairyland's Talisman: the Rainbow Feather.'

She repeated the words Witch Whisper had told her just before she left the Tree: 'A gorgeous feather imbued with every colour imaginable and as long as a fairy's arm.'

'It sounds beautiful,' Melody gushed.

'It does,' Silky agreed. 'But it could be anywhere in Fairyland. Finding it won't be easy . . .'

Pinx's eyes had grown very wide.

'Yes, it will,' she said.

'What do you mean?' Silky asked excitedly. 'You've seen it?'

'Seen it?' exclaimed Pinx. 'I *found* that

plume. It's beautiful – exactly how you described it!'

'This is incredible!' Silky gasped. 'So you have it?'

Pinx cocked her head. She had an odd look in her eyes.

'Not *exactly* . . .'

'Then where is it?' Silky cried.

'It's . . . um . . . exactly in the centre of the bodice of Princess Twilleria's Sweet Centennial dress,' Pinx admitted.

'That's perfect!' Melody chirped. 'You can just take out the Feather and sew another in its place!'

Pinx shot her quite possibly the most withering glare ever.

'Or . . . not,' Melody mumbled, briefly considering turning back into a music box.

'Maybe you don't understand,' Pinx explained. 'That plume is magnificent. The entire dress is built around it. There is *no way*

I'm taking it apart before the party.'

Silky took a deep breath.

'Pinx,' she said gently, 'I know how important that dress is to you, but I don't think it's safe to have the Feather anywhere Talon can get at it –'

'It isn't!' Pinx interjected. 'It's in a vault in the castle and it'll stay there until the party.'

'But what about *at* the party?' asked Silky. 'How do we know Talon won't try to get it there?'

'Oh, please,' Pinx rolled her eyes. 'Princess Twilleria's Sweet Centennial is a VIP pink-carpet event. Only the elite of the elite of the *elite* will be there. Believe me, the Troll won't be on the list.'

The other fairies just looked at Pinx.

'Although . . .' Pinx realised, '. . . I don't suppose he'd really pay attention to the list . . .'

'Pinx . . .' Silky began.

She knew that Pinx wouldn't like what she

was about to say.

'No, wait. I have an idea.' Pinx said.

She looked at her four friends, scrutinising them: Melody with her ponytail and her simple light-blue V-neck; Petal in her skirt and top; Bizzy in her crazy coloured clothes and bangles. Pinx's eyes rested on Silky and she took a deep breath.

'OK,' she declared, as if she had won an argument with herself. 'I can swing tickets for the four of you to come to the Sweet Centennial.'

'You can?' exclaimed Bizzy ecstatically.

'Yes,' said Pinx, 'and then if anything happens – which it won't, but if it does – we'll all be there. The team.'

'At the Sweet Centennial?' Melody's eyes danced with delight.

'Yes . . . but you have to promise you'll let me dress you,' Pinx insisted. 'If you're coming with me, you have to look fantastic – better than everyone except Twilleria. And me, of course.'

'You're going to make us dresses?' Melody gasped. 'We get to wear Pinx dresses?'

'Oh wow,' Bizzy gushed. 'We'll look like celebrities. We'll hang out with celebrities! We'll *be* celebrities!'

Only Silky hadn't said anything.

'Silky?' asked Petal, turning to her.

Four pairs of eager eyes stared anxiously at Silky, waiting for her response.

'I don't know . . .' Silky began. 'I mean, if we know where the Feather is, shouldn't we just get it and take it straight back to the Tree?'

Petal, Melody and Bizzy's faces fell. Pinx looked as if she was going to be sick. And yet . . . they didn't argue. Silky realised that they were willing to take her advice. Even though it would make them miserable, even though they would be horribly disappointed, they were willing to put the mission first.

They were her team, and Silky didn't want to let them down.

'But if it's really going to be in the castle vault until the party, and we can all be there to guard it . . .' she said with a smile.

Silky's friends beamed at her.

'You mean . . .?' Pinx urged.

'I mean I think you have some dresses to make,' Silky grinned.

'*Yes!*' Melody screamed.

Bizzy reached out, putting her hand in the middle of the group.

'To the Totally Tremendous, Talon-Trouncing, Talisman-Toting Team!' she cried.

The other fairies reached out and placed their hands on top of Bizzy's.

'To the team!' they cried.

Then they flew off to Pinx's studio to model for their dresses and prepare for what would surely be the most fabulous night of their lives.

Chapter Ten

The Sweet Centennial Ball

'Look at us!' Bizzy cried. 'We're a Bevy of Brilliantly Bewitching Beauties!'

She, Pinx, Silky, Petal and Melody were riding in the back of a Flying Flowerferry as it soared through the air, pulled by a team of pink-tailed dragonflies: it was the only way Pinx would allow them to travel to the Sweet Centennial.

Despite Pinx's hectic schedule of clients over the last twenty-four hours, she had somehow also managed to completely dedicate herself to making her friends look as glamorous as possible for the magical evening. The final result? Five fabulous fairies in a cacophony of every shade of pink under the sun, their flounced skirts and tailored bodices a wild explosion of feathers, flowers, pufflepoofs and ruffellettas. They looked absolutely beautiful.

'Just promise me one thing,' Pinx cautioned as their Flowerferry pulled up to the entrance. 'Please don't embarrass me. The celebrities here are my clients and my friends. Just . . . try to be calm.'

'Of course!' cried Bizzy, and everyone else agreed.

Pinx took a deep breath and opened the Flowerferry door. A huge, screaming throng was gathered around the pink carpet. Pinx worked the crowd expertly, waving and smiling for the seemingly endless photographs. Silky, Bizzy, Petal and Melody were completely overwhelmed and stuck close together behind Pinx, following her lead. Then Bizzy noticed something a few metres ahead.

'Wow!' she hissed in Pinx's ear. 'Is that Marisolode? I *love* her!'

'Yes, it is,' Pinx whisper-hissed through her smile. 'And I can introduce you later if you just . . . Bizzy?'

But Bizzy was gone.

'Marisolode!' Bizzy screeched as she flew up to her favourite star. 'I am your biggest, biggest fan! A Major Marisolode Maniac! Can you sign . . .' she looked around desperately for something her idol could sign, ' . . . my arm?'

'Hi Maris!' Pinx swooped in, bubbling with everything's-OK charm as she took Bizzy's arm. 'I'm so sorry about my cousin. We'll see you inside, OK?'

Pinx whisked Bizzy off down the pink carpet, mouthing pointedly over her shoulder to the actress, 'She's not well.'

Marisolode nodded with understanding and gave Pinx a sympathetic thumbs-up.

'What are you doing?' Pinx hissed to Bizzy once they were out of earshot and back with their other friends. 'Did everyone pay attention? Because what Bizzy has just done is the perfect example of what *not* to do tonight.'

But the other girls weren't listening. They had reached the ballroom and were breathless with wonder.

'Wow,' gasped Silky, speaking for all of them.

The ballroom itself was an enormous pink flower, planted on the day of the Princess's birth and carefully tended for a hundred years until it was large enough to house this event. Tables covered in layers of crinolined skirts and sprays of dazzling blooms dotted the floor. A dazzling pyramid of multicoloured presents towered at one side of the room. The air danced with the sweeps and swirls of gowned fairies and tuxedoed wing-o-lytes whirling to the soft music of the band.

'Thank you, Pinx,' murmured Melody. 'I'll

remember this for the rest of my life.'

'You're welcome,' said Pinx. 'I'm glad I could share this with all of you . . . hey . . . where's Petal?'

Before anyone could reply, a strikingly beautiful fairy approached, her nose high in the air.

'Pinx!' she cried, and fluttered over, air-kissing Pinx once on each cheek.

'Duchess Eleanorian,' Pinx cooed.

'Duchess Elean–' Bizzy began to squeal, but Pinx elbowed her in the ribs.

'So good to see someone of the proper class in here,' the Duchess oozed, leaning closer to whisper in Pinx's ear, 'I swear I saw that fairy *talking* to the *flowers*!' She nodded towards one of the tables.

'*Really*?' Pinx said through clenched teeth. 'How odd!'

The minute the Duchess left, Pinx made a beeline for Petal, who was indeed having a long, involved conversation with the rose display on table eight.

'*Petal!*' Pinx hissed. 'You must stop now. OK? *Now.*'

'But these roses are getting awfully hungry. Do you know when their dinner's coming?' Petal asked.

Pinx could only splutter.

Meanwhile, Silky was feeling as if she was in an enchanted dream. Calyx, a handsome wing-o-lyte, had asked her to dance and she was suddenly swept into the swirl and twirl of dancers filling the air. It was so glorious that for a moment she forgot all about the threat to the Enchanted World.

Then the band stopped and a lone trumpeter blew a flourish. The Princess was coming! Silky said goodbye to Calyx and flew back down to be with her friends for the big moment.

The entire room hushed. All the fairies and wing-o-lytes drifted to the outer edges of the flower-ballroom. A spotlight shone on the floor. As a drum roll grew in intensity, a hole opened in the floor of the ballroom. A giant platform, emblazoned with the words 'Sweet Centennial', rose into the centre of the room. The drum roll stopped and POOF! The top of the platform rose to reveal Princess Twilleria herself, who spread her wings and soared upwards into the spotlight. Her light-brown curls and chocolate skin were the perfect complement to Pinx's magnificent dress – a symphony of fuchsia, carnation, salmon, coral, cherry blossom and magenta.

But the bodice . . . it was the bodice that made every jaw in the room drop to the floor. It was constructed only of feathers, with a central plume that reached from the Princess's waist to the bottom of her throat. It glistened with a thousand colours and seemed to glow

Sweet Centennial

with its own inner light. It was breathtaking.

'That's it,' Silky whispered. 'The Rainbow Feather.'

'It has to be!' gasped Melody. 'Look at your necklace!'

Sure enough, the necklace Witch Whisper had given Silky was now glowing a deep crimson.

Princess Twilleria gave a majestic twirl and everyone in the room gasped, bursting into applause over the wonder of the Princess in her incredible dress. Twilleria bowed humbly. As she rose, she looked at Pinx, winked and mouthed 'Thanks'.

'Did you see that?!' Bizzy whispered ecstatically, nudging Pinx. 'The Princess spoke to you!'

'Of course she did,' Pinx said nonchalantly, but even she couldn't hide the proud grin that now lit up her face.

Silky smiled at the sight, glad she had

agreed to let everyone stay for the party.

'What happens now?' whispered Melody.

'The Princess will choose a wing-o-lyte for her first dance as a Sweet Centennial,' Pinx said. 'It's a huge honour for the wing-o-lyte she picks.'

The crowd waited in hushed awe as the Princess surveyed the available wing-o-lytes, all preening to be noticed. But just as she was about to make her choice . . .

RRRIP! The side of the giant flower-ballroom was torn open.

'No!' Petal gasped.

Petal was horrified by the yawning tear in this living flower, but Silky knew that worse was to come.

'It's Talon!' she yelled.

Even as she said his name, the Troll burst in through the gash in the plant, clinging to an enchanted vine. Swinging low, he tore the Rainbow Feather from the bodice of

Twilleria's beautiful dress. Missing its centrepiece, the dress fell to shreds around Twilleria's ankles, leaving the Princess in only her slip.

A single cry rang out, but it didn't come from the Princess.

'*Nobody destroys my dress!*' shrieked a livid Pinx.

With a blood-curdling scream, she raced after Talon.

Chapter Eleven

The Chase

It only took a moment for the initial shock to wear off and then the party descended into chaos.

'My *dress*!' Princess Twilleria squealed, falling to the floor and desperately trying to gather the loose feathers, frills and fabric back around her body. Several fairies rushed to her aid, while hordes of others tried to grab the glorious odds and ends of Pinx's creation for themselves, fighting over the prettiest pieces.

At first they only wrestled for the strewn shreds of Twilleria's ruined dress, but as the pandemonium grew, the fairies started ripping at *each other's* dresses. In no time, hundreds of scavengers were rolling around in their slips, clawing at one another's outfits, each trying to gather the most magnificent horde of fabric and frills. Feathers, sequinolines and pufflepoofs soon turned the entire ballroom into a snow globe of flying frills.

Silky, Petal, Bizzy and Melody were flying around in the middle of it all, trying to keep away from the mayhem.

'This is insane,' cried Petal, dodging a sequinolined sheath.

'It's a blizzard of blustery baubles!' cried Bizzy, delighted, as she caught a huge clot of delicious, sweet pufflegoo in her mouth.

'I think it's beautiful,' mused Melody.

The Sweet Centennial had become a massive frenzy of flying fairies, wing-o-lytes, creampuffs, fabrics and feathery frills. Within seconds, nearly every guest was coated in pufflegoo from the creampuffs, which attracted the flying feathers like glue. Soon the elite of the elite of the *elite* looked like frosted flamingos in the wake of a tornado.

Silky squinted against the debris in the air, flitting up and down as she searched for the best spot.

'I can't see anything!' she exclaimed, 'I can't see Pinx or Talon!'

But a moment later she certainly *heard* Pinx. The furious fairy had caught up with Talon and was letting him know exactly how she felt.

'How *dare* you destroy my dress?' she screamed.

Pinx pulled Talon from his vine and lunged for the Feather, but the Troll grabbed her by the wrist.

'Another feisty fairy,' he growled. 'How nice.'

As he started to chant in Trollish, the air cleared just enough for Silky to see her friend caught in Talon's grip. It was the same grip in which he'd caught Silky back in the Land of Mine-All-Mine. In a flash, Silky realised the truth.

'Pinx!' she shrieked. 'Don't let him touch you! His magic will only work if he's touching you!'

'She's lying!' Talon hissed, but Pinx saw the uncertainty in his eyes and knew Silky was right.

Pinx scrunched up her eyes and turned invisible, which surprised Talon just enough for Pinx to pull away. Talon hopped on to a large buffet platter of party snacks and enchanted it to fly. Then, with the Feather clutched tight in his fist, he soared towards the rip he had made in the wall of the ballroom flower.

'I'll stop him!' Bizzy cried, raising her arms in the air. 'Slithell-little-hiss-n-fiddle!' she shouted, throwing out her arms.

POOF! A large rake now lay in the middle of the floor.

'A rake?' Silky asked incredulously. 'You made a *rake*?'

'Bit of a Bizzy Blunder,' Bizzy admitted. 'I wanted a giant *snake* to grab Talon in its mouth!'

'I think I like the rake more,' Melody said with a grimace.

'Girls!' Silky shouted. 'Talon's getting away with the Rainbow Feather!'

With no snake to stop him, Talon's enchanted platter sped him towards the gash in the ballroom wall.

'Farewell, my fine fairy friends!' Talon called as he soared towards freedom.

But before he could get away, several of the fairies who were wrestling for dress pieces stepped backwards on to the teeth of the rake. They weren't hurt, but their weight tipped the rake handle straight up in the air . . . where it *smacked* straight into Talon, sending him and his plate flying in opposite directions.

'Told you I liked the rake,' Melody chirped.

Still clutching the Feather, Talon got to his

feet and ran for the main door, dodging flying
fabric and slipping on puddles of pufflegoo.
Silky suddenly saw her chance.

'I've got him!' she cried.

She shot a beam of light into the tower of
Twilleria's presents, which tumbled down like
a multicoloured avalanche, cutting off Talon's
escape.

'Give us the Feather, Talon!' Silky cried,
soaring towards him.

'I'll destroy it first!' Talon howled, ducking away from Silky and racing in the other direction to find a new escape route.

'Allow me,' said Petal.

She called out to the floral centrepieces. One by one, the artfully arranged bouquets lifted themselves by their leaves and sped, spider-like, towards Talon, worming their way around his ankles, legs, torso and arms, and pinning him down with their thorns.

'Yes!' cried Petal.

She soared down to pluck the Feather from Talon's tethered arms, but just before she arrived, Talon mumbled something in Trollish. His crystal flared and the flowers turned brown, shrivelling away from their captive.

'No!' gasped a horrified Petal.

She swooped down to gather the dying flowers in her arms as Talon ran away. Hearing her cries, the other girls flew to her side.

'They only came after Talon because I asked them to . . . and now they're dying,' said Petal, her voice breaking as she choked out the end of her thought. 'I killed them.'

She started to sob, but Melody quickly came to her aid.

'It's OK, Petal,' she cooed. 'They're only partially burned. I can help.'

She leaned in close to the blossoms and lifted her voice in a gentle lullaby, so beautiful that it gave them strength.

Colour miraculously flowed back into the leaves and petals, and the wilted blooms grew larger than ever.

'See?' Melody told Petal. 'They'll be fine.'

'But the Rainbow Feather won't,' said Silky. 'Look!'

She pointed to the other end of the room, where Talon had almost scaled the tower of presents that blocked the main door.

'My turn!' cried Pinx, but Silky held her back.

'No!' Silky demanded. 'It's time to start working together!'

As she spoke, an idea burst into Silky's mind.

'I have it!' she squealed, and drew her friends together, desperate to speak as fast as she could think.

Within moments, they were ready.

'Hey, Talon!' Silky cried out, soaring into the air behind him.

The Troll only turned for a split second, but that was all it took. Petal had been whispering to the giant bloom that was the ballroom itself, and the bloom now obeyed. One of its sides slammed into Talon and threw him off balance as he teetered back into the room. While Talon reeled, Silky shot a flash of light in front of his eyes, blinding him for several seconds. As he staggered forwards, he slipped

on Melody, who had transformed herself into a large sheet of ice on the floor. Shocked, Talon slid uncontrollably across the Melody-ice-sheet on his bottom, as Bizzy recited a spell to make . . .

'A *cake*?' Pinx cried.

That's exactly what Bizzy had made: an enormous, pink-frosted, sugary delight of a cake, larger than ten fairies. It was impressive, but . . .

'It was supposed to be a *cage*!' Pinx wailed.

Bizzy shrugged apologetically, but Talon was already sliding towards them and there was nothing to do but continue with the plan. The invisible Pinx pushed the giant cake into Talon's path and he stretched out his arms to push it away, but the cake was far too big.

SPLOOSH! Talon shot headfirst into the cake. Chocolate sponge and fuchsia icing spattered the already-feathered-and-creamed party guests, as well as Silky, Bizzy, Petal,

Melody and Pinx.

As for Talon, he was completely trapped inside the cake. Only his feet and hands stuck out, including the hand that gripped the Rainbow Feather. Silky plucked the Feather neatly away and the five fairies raced for the door as fast as they could fly.

Soon they were out of the ballroom and on their way back to the Faraway Tree.

'Good idea to change the plan,' Silky congratulated Bizzy. 'If he'd been in a cage, he'd have been casting spells all over the place. What gave you the idea for the cake?'

Bizzy looked over at Pinx, who just shook her head and rolled her eyes.

'She's just Bizzy,' Pinx said. 'It's what makes her the right person for our team.'

And she and Bizzy shared a grin as they all soared away.

Chapter Twelve

The Faraway Fairies

Later, when they were safely back in the Faraway Tree, Silky, Melody, Petal, Bizzy and Pinx watched as Witch Whisper returned the Rainbow Feather to its proper place in the Vault. Although there were many more Talismans to recover, and the danger to the Faraway Tree and the Enchanted World was still very real, everyone in the Tree felt that the Rainbow Feather was a sign of great things to come.

Witch Whisper declared that they should have a party in honour of the returned Talisman and the Tree's four newest residents. Melody, Petal, Bizzy and Pinx had all decided to stay on and continue with the mission. They were excited about the festivities and eager to meet everyone. Only Silky seemed preoccupied.

'Silky, are you OK?' Melody asked.

The other fairies' faces mirrored her concern. It wasn't like Silky to be so distracted.

'I'm fine,' Silky said. 'I just . . . I'll catch up with you later, OK?'

She flew off without another word.

Hours later, Silky was sitting all alone in her and Zuni's favourite place. It was a hidden alcove on a remote branch near the top of the Tree, where a full, thick canopy of leaves created a dome of perfect darkness. Silky was able to light it just enough to shed a soft glow. It was the perfect light to think by . . . and all she could muster in her mood.

Slowly, several branches at the edge of the alcove shifted apart and Witch Whisper pushed her way inside. Although no one but Silky and Zuni knew about this place, Silky wasn't surprised to see the older woman. Witch Whisper said nothing. She just sat next to Silky and waited.

After a while, Silky spoke.

'I don't think I can forgive myself,' she whispered softly. 'My best friends have left their homes, put themselves in terrible danger and given up everything . . . and it's all because of me.'

'Your friends are here because they *want* to be here,' Witch Whisper corrected her. 'They want to do their part to help the Enchanted World.'

'Which wouldn't be in trouble if it wasn't for me,' Silky stressed.

She fell silent and Witch Whisper sat with her, saying nothing until Silky spoke again.

'How can I trust myself again?' said Silky in a small voice. 'I didn't think twice about going to the Land of Mine-All-Mine by myself. I've gone alone to Lands a hundred times before. But it turned out to be such a huge mistake. The girls all look to me like I'm in charge, but I don't think I can be. How can I be sure that even the smallest decision I make isn't going to be a disaster?'

This was the question that had been weighing most heavily on Silky's mind. It was what was keeping her away from the party, her friends and all the celebrations.

Witch Whisper sighed.

'How do you trust yourself again?' she asked. 'Because you have to. You made a mistake. We all do. This one had big consequences, but you're facing them and working to make it better. If you just keep kicking yourself over what you did wrong, you'll never move forward . . . and pretty soon you'll have spent centuries shut away in a cottage in the bottom of the Faraway Tree, so cut off that everyone around you thinks you're a doddering old fool.'

Silky looked at Witch Whisper, but the witch was staring straight ahead, lost in her own thoughts.

'You made a big mistake too?' Silky asked softly.

'I did,' Witch Whisper admitted, then smiled, turning to face Silky. 'But that is a story for another time. Just believe me, you'll trust yourself again. And when you're unsure, draw strength from your friends, myself included. We trust you.' Witch Whisper rose. 'Come on. I know four fairies who are very anxious to see you. They're lovely by the way. Although Pinx doesn't like my cloak . . .'

Witch Whisper extended her hand and Silky took it with a smile. Together they left the alcove; Witch Whisper soared up to visit Cluecatcher while Silky flew down towards her home. Just as she got there . . .

'*Surprise!*' Bizzy, Melody, Petal and Pinx burst out of the leaves next to Silky, making her scream in shock and then giggle in delight.

'What are you doing?' Silky asked. 'I thought you'd be at the party . . .'

'We couldn't have a party without you,' insisted Melody.

That was when she saw it: a newly built treehouse behind her four friends.

'Wow . . .' Silky gasped. 'What did you do?'

'Come and see!' Melody giggled, dragging Silky inside.

Silky couldn't believe it. Her tiny, one-roomed treehouse had been replaced by the perfect home for five fairies. It was large and open, with a huge main room, a giant kitchen, five bedrooms with interconnecting doors, and slides and poles connecting all the levels.

'This is incredible!' Silky cried. 'How did you do all this?'

'My spells don't *always* go wrong,' Bizzy chirped.

'But when they *did*, Zuni helped us rebuild,' Petal added, smiling.

'I love it,' Silky said. 'Thank you. Thank you so much.'

'You don't think that's it, do you?' Pinx said.

'Show her, Bizzy!' added Melody.

'Festoonillia, Festoonalia, Festoonamareda!' Bizzy cried, throwing out her arms. '*Now* the party can begin!'

The whole treehouse was transformed into an almost exact replica of Princess Twilleria's Sweet Centennial Ball . . . *before* everything went wrong.

'What?' Silky spluttered. 'What is this?'

But before anyone could answer, fairies and wing-o-lytes poured in, along with Zuni, Dame Washalot, Misty the Unicorn, Dido the Dragon . . . even the Angry Pixie rushed in with the other Faraway-Tree residents. A band began to play and, just like in the flower-

ballroom, the sky was filled with twirling couples.

Melody, Pinx, Bizzy and Petal beamed, but Silky was just stunned. She stared at the crowd.

'Oh wow . . . that's Marisolode!' she gasped, spotting the famous movie star in the crowd. 'That's *Princess Twilleria*! Here – in our home! How did you do this?'

'They wanted to come,' Petal said. 'We're having a party. They missed out on their party.'

'And Twilleria really wanted her party,' Pinx said, rolling her eyes.

As Silky grinned, Pinx noticed something behind her.

'Whoa, whoa, whoa!' she cried. 'Bizzy, that's a *magenta* streamer. I thought we said all the streamers would be *coral*?'

The fairies just laughed, but stopped as Calyx, the particularly handsome wing-o-lyte, approached Silky.

'I was hoping we might continue our dance,' Calyx said.

Silky beamed at her friends. 'Of course,' she replied, and he whisked her into the air.

They hadn't been dancing for more than a second when Zuni somersaulted into the air to tap on Calyx's shoulder.

'Sorry, my friend!' Zuni said as gravity carried him back to the ground. 'I'm cutting in!'

Calyx bowed out gracefully and Silky watched him as he flew off into the crowd, then she landed next to Zuni. She smiled at her friend, an impish look in her eye.

'Oh come on,' Zuni scoffed. 'What – you like him?'

Silky just laughed.

'You're not jealous, are you?' she asked with a smile.

'Don't even know the meaning of the

word,' he said, then paused and added earnestly, 'I'm glad you're home safely.'

'Thanks,' said Silky. 'Me too.'

'Want to dance?' Zuni asked, holding out his arms.

'I'd love to,' Silky replied.

But before she could even take Zuni's hand, Witch Whisper burst into the cottage.

'Silky, Petal, Pinx, Bizzy, Melody!' Witch Whisper called, and the fairies raced over to her. 'Cluecatcher has sensed the next Land, but he can't tell what it is yet.'

'When does the Land get here?' Silky asked.

'Very soon,' Witch Whisper said with a smile. 'But there is enough time for you to enjoy your party and get these fairy guests back to Fairyland before it floats away from the Tree. Goodnight.'

She left and the girls looked at one another excitedly.

'I wonder where we get to go next,' said
Pinx eagerly.

'Think we'll be ready?' Melody said.

Silky looked at her four friends, each of
them so incredibly different and so incredibly
talented. Any one of them would be a force to
be reckoned with, but together ...

'Of course!' Silky beamed. 'We're
unstoppable.'

The five fairies hugged one another and then soared back to the party. Somewhere out there, Talon was getting ready to enter the next Land and take its Talisman. But the Faraway Fairies were ready for him, each of them eager for their next thrilling adventure . . .

If you can't wait for another exciting
adventure with Silky and her fairy
friends, here's a sneak preview . . .

Enid Blyton's

ENCHANTED
WORLD

Melody and the
Enchanted Harp

For fun and activities, go to
www.blyton.com/enchantedworld

Chapter One
Calm in Chaos

'AAAHHH!' wailed Pinx as a fierce blast of wind blew a flurry of butterblooms off the dress she was creating for Petal, who stood patiently on Pinx's fitting pedestal.

'Silky!' Pinx huffed as she flew around the room chasing the flowers, 'I just pinned those on!'

'Sorry, Pinx!' Silky cried over her shoulder, but she was already far across the main room of the fairies' treehouse, riding behind Zuni on the back of Misty the Unicorn. As Misty soared through the air, her mighty wings beat gust after gust. Although that caused a problem for Pinx, it was heavenly for Silky. She loved the feeling of the wind streaking through her long, blonde hair as Zuni urged Misty to dive, twirl and perform all her most impressive tricks.

'This one's brand new,' Zuni grinned.

Silky screamed with delight as Misty executed a perfect loop-the-loop, the wind from which sent the butterblooms flying all over again. Pinx's face turned as pink as her zigzag pigtails as she roared in frustration, which of course made Petal laugh out loud.

'Oh, Pinx, it's OK,' Petal said in her most soothing voice. 'Let me help.'

She flew off the platform to chase the blooms. But although the two fairies tried, it was impossible to chase down all the butterblooms that filled the room. Several blooms floated down to Bizzy, who was very carefully opening the oven door. Her wild, black curls were spattered with dabs of flour, butter and spellulose, her secret ingredient for Magical Message Muffins, which she had been trying unsuccessfully to bake all day.

'I think the key,' said Bizzy as she gingerly

took out the twelfth muffin pan of the afternoon, 'is to be silent and still while I say the final spell. Muffle-wuffle-rise-n-puff–AAAAH!'

A flurry of butterblooms floated down from above, followed closely by a swooping twosome of Petal and Pinx.

'I've got them!' both fairies shouted.

Bizzy looked up to see her friends dive-bombing towards her, screamed and raised the muffin tin above her head like a shield – a motion that sent the muffins springing out of the tin and on to the floor. Muffins on the floor were an irresistible treat to the crowd of birds, squirrels and other small animals that liked to stay close to Petal. Just as the birds lunged for the muffins, Bizzy's improperly finished spell took effect, turning the treats into a dozen *puffins*.

The puffins squawked angrily, then waddled and flew around the room, eagerly searching for any morsels of fish.

This was life in the Faraway Fairies' treehouse. Ever since Silky had gathered her best friends to live in the Faraway Tree and join her on a mission to retrieve its life-giving Talismans, every day was a whirlwind of giddy chaos, with friends like Zuni and Misty, not to mention a rotating menagerie of Petal's animal friends coming round to join in the excitement.

Only one fairy seemed completely serene in the midst of the insanity. Melody floated in the middle of the room and danced, unaffected by Misty's tricks, the snowstorm of blooms or even the sudden appearance of puffins.

'One, two . . .' she counted as she performed a perfect pirouette, moved into an arabesque and then did a double scissor-kick. Without missing a beat of the song lilting through her head, she deftly ducked out of the way of Misty, who was still carrying Zuni and Silky through her favourite tricks.

'Sorry about that, Melody,' Zuni called, but Melody didn't respond.

'Melody?' Silky said.

Melody didn't answer her either. She just screwed up her green eyes, concentrating even harder, then flew straight up in the air and spun around ten times in a row – a decuple twirliette – an almost unheard-of achievement among Twinkletune Fairies. Melody's friends would have been stunned if they had noticed, but none of them had. Melody didn't mind. She just allowed herself a small smile and then turned her attention back to Silky and Zuni.

'Sorry,' Melody said. 'I just wanted to make the step perfect.'

Pinx and Petal had finished gathering up the butterblooms and Pinx was back to working on her latest masterpiece, but she turned to Melody with a grimace.

'I don't get it,' she declared. 'If you need to

concentrate, why not practise in your room?'

But Melody was already working on another dance routine, and sang out her answer to the tune running through her head: 'I dance my best when I'm happy, and I'm at my happiest when I'm with all of you.'

Bizzy used her foot to close the oven door on her latest muffin attempt and then grabbed a puffin, adding it to the squawking foursome already wriggling in her arms.

'But aren't we a Dilly of Decided Distractions?' she asked.

As if to prove her point, a puffin squirmed out of her grasp and flew straight at Melody, who grabbed it by its wings.

'You're not *very* distracting,' Melody declared, incorporating the puffin into her dance by spinning it twice around before giving it a deep dip. 'Besides,' she continued, twirling the puffin back to Bizzy, 'I can do anything I set my mind to.'

There was something in Melody's voice as she spoke that made Silky pay attention. It was a determination. Silky had heard it in her friend before, even when they were kids, but Melody had such a happy-go-lucky nature that it was easy to forget this other side of her. Intrigued, Silky flew off Misty's back to take a closer look. She saw the same Melody as always: long orange ponytail, open green eyes and that straight-backed stance that Silky had always attributed to years of dancing. But now that she thought about it, maybe Melody's posture wasn't just training. Maybe it was a sign of her inner steel.

Silky smiled, looking at her friend with new admiration, but before she could say anything, there was a knock at the door. Silky opened it to reveal an enormous head teetering on a tiny body. The head was dominated by a shockingly large nose that ran all the way from the top of the forehead to the bottom of the chin, and two radar-dish ears that rotated quickly, picking up every sound within range. This was Cluecatcher, and there was only one reason why he would show up at the treehouse with such an anxious look in his eight eyes. Silky lit up with excitement.

'There's a new Land coming to the top of the Tree!' she gasped.

A wrinkled old woman cloaked in black stepped out from behind Cluecatcher.

'Yes, there is,' Witch Whisper confirmed.

She stepped inside with Cluecatcher as all the other fairies, Zuni and Misty stopped what they were doing to gather around.

'It's the Land of Music,' Witch Whisper continued, 'and its Talisman is the Enchanted Harp.'

Melody gasped audibly.

'The Land of Music?' she cried. 'But I can't –'

Melody suddenly seemed to realise that

everyone was looking at her in concern. She forced a smile and tried to sound positive.

'I can't wait!' she continued. 'I've always *dreamed* of visiting the Land of Music.'

She must have sounded convincing because everyone turned back to Witch Whisper. Everyone except Silky. Melody smiled wider to show her friend that she was fine.

'You all understand what's at stake,' Witch Whisper continued. 'The Talismans that tie the Faraway Tree to each Land of the Enchanted World must be returned to our Vault. They are the Tree's life force. Without them, the Tree will die. And if they fall into the wrong hands . . .'

'*Talon's* hands,' Pinx interrupted venomously.

She still hadn't forgiven the evil Troll for ruining the dress that she had made for Princess Twilleria's Sweet Centennial Ball.

'He'll be after the Harp,' Witch Whisper warned. 'He's desperate to control the gateway to the Enchanted World.'

DING!

'Oh!' Bizzy cried, and zipped back to the oven, where she gingerly removed the muffin tin, closed her eyes and concentrated, chanting, 'Muffle-wuffle-rise-n-puffle!'

POOF! The muffins puffed up to twice their size.

'It worked!' Bizzy cheered. 'And now we can finally read our Majorly Monumental Magic Muffin Message!'

She ripped open a piping-hot muffin and pulled out a small scroll from inside. Bizzy managed to unroll the warm note and read it aloud: 'Tread lightly where you don't belong, lest sorrow be your only song.'

Pinx wrinkled up her nose.

'What does that mean?' she asked.

'It means . . .' Melody began nervously, but an excited Bizzy cut her off.

'It means we shouldn't be Hopelessly Hapless Homebodies when we have a

Massively Momentous Mission in the Land of Music!' she cried. 'Let's go!'

Bizzy flew off towards the Ladder at the top of the Tree, with the other fairies following close behind. Melody came last, and when Silky turned, she could see her friend's normally pale face had turned absolutely white. Silky flew close to Melody.

'Is everything OK?' she asked gently.

But as soon as Melody heard Silky's concern, she banished all doubt from her face.

'It's great!' Melody beamed. 'I'm right behind you.' But Silky wasn't reassured. Something about the Land of Music was bothering Melody horribly, but *what*? What could be so terrible that Melody couldn't share it with her closest friends?

EGMONT PRESS: ETHICAL PUBLISHING

Egmont Press is about turning writers into successful authors and children into passionate readers – producing books that enrich and entertain. As a responsible children's publisher, we go even further, considering the world in which our consumers are growing up.

Safety First
Naturally, all of our books meet legal safety requirements. But we go further than this; every book with play value is tested to the highest standards – if it fails, it's back to the drawing-board.

Made Fairly
We are working to ensure that the workers involved in our supply chain – the people that make our books – are treated with fairness and respect.

Responsible Forestry
We are committed to ensuring all our papers come from environmentally and socially responsible forest sources.

For more information, please visit our website at
www.egmont.co.uk/ethicalpublishing

The Forest Stewardship Council (FSC) is an international, non-governmental organisation dedicated to promoting responsible management of the world's forests. FSC operates a system of forest certification and product labelling that allows consumers to identify wood and wood-based products from well-managed forests.

For more information about the FSC, please visit their website at www.fsc-uk.org

FSC
Mixed Sources
Product group from well-managed forests and other controlled sources

Cert no. TT-COC-2063
www.fsc.org
© 1996 Forest Stewardship Council